FATHER FIGURE

SUSPENSEFUL TALES OF FATHERHOOD

DAN B. FIERCE

Trigger Warning:

This is Horror.

Some of the themes in this book may upset sensitive readers. Those themes include but are not limited to child endangerment and murder, suicide, abuse, animal abuse, mental illness, violence, gore, and many other extremes.

This is not the book for those looking for feel-good stories. While there may be some wholesome and satisfying endings, make no mistake that the genre is built to frighten and make the reader think. No one is safe from life's horrors; not adults, children, or animals. That may be a brash way to see it, but it is, unfortunately, reality.

Also, note that these stories are works of fiction. Any similarities between real people, places, or events are coincidental. It is also absolutely no reflection upon my own father.

As the author, I try to limit the scope of these experiences because I know the trauma involved can be very impactful. That said, buyer beware. Go into this book knowing that there are unsettling things contained herein.

You have been warned.

This. Is. Horror

Oh, and one final trigger warning: I am proud member of the LGBTQIA+ community. There are gay themes in here. If reading my book would be considered a form of support in the reader's mind, or go against their beliefs, then they should take note and skip over it. I refuse to apologize for being who I am.

Never again.

TABLE OF CONTENTS

*This book is dedicated to the man who helped make
me who I am today. Even if I didn't see it then.*

I love you, Dad.

"Anyone can be a father, but it takes someone special to be a dad, and that's why I call you dad, because you are so special to me. You taught me the game and you taught me how to play it right."

- Wade Boggs

"An almost perfect relationship with his father was the earthly root of all his wisdom."

- C.S. Lewis

"He adopted a role called being a father so that his child would have something mythical and infinitely important: a protector."

- Tom Wolfe

It's funny. When my father was still alive, and I was in my rebellious teen years, he and I butted heads often. What boy didn't? He was a difficult man to read. I was probably the same. He and I were too much alike at times.

He had a love for spaghetti westerns, sports, and action flicks. His favorite author was Louis L'Amour. I also remember seeing him weep on a rare occasion.

He loved to play "Dirty Rat" and taught me how to play "Twenty-one" and "Blackjack" to pass time when we were camping on rainy days. We'd split the till of pocket change he'd amassed, use it to make our bets, and then return it all to the same jar for the next night. We'd play horseshoes, He taught me how to fish, and how to clean them.

He gave me an appreciation of nature and travel. He taught me a good work ethic and lamented my uncanny ability to procrastinate. (I still haven't shaken that. Sorry, Dad.) He was a wonderful provider, even if he didn't do it alone. I wanted for nothing. Except Levi's. Wranglers just weren't the same. (Then I grew up and no longer cared about labels, just as he said I shouldn't.)

He's been gone for thirty years now, and I have so much to say to him. That's why I made this book and dedicated it to him.

Yes, they are horror stories. No, my father was not an awful person in the slightest. Let me make that perfectly clear. I was blessed by God to have that man in my life. Why it took me so many years to bring myself to appreciate him is beyond me. Maybe it's that procrastination of mine rearing its ugly side. Not everybody gets so lucky.

That's why I penned this collection; not to make readers scared of father figures, but as my way of honoring mine. Isn't that what we're supposed to do when they deserve it? I don't know whether it's truly "horror" or not, but I do know that, as I wrote it, it made me feel. I hope that everyone feels it as deeply as I did.

THE LETTER

Pulling into the cemetery, I park next to the resting place of a good part of my matriarchal family. I get out and explore the ground-hugging markers to locate my relatives. Kneeling, I peel away last fall's dead leaves clinging to the marble like mourning friends. The next to go is the spreading crabgrass along the edges. I don't visit these plots as often as a good person should.

My chest tightens, the lump in my throat growing, as I prune away the invasive vegetation. The earth releases a petrichor that satisfies me as my family's markers are now more visible.

"The caretakers must not weed-eat," I mutter, both a curse and a musing at the state of things. "They need to do a better job."

One by one, I repeat the ritualistic process. Finally, I stand tall and nod at my contribution. Many relatives that I knew, and some I didn't, populate this little section of the quiet landscape. The strangers jigsawed betwixt them make my efforts look discriminatory. A small pang of guilt erupts within me, that I don't treat their headstones to the same spa treatment. It vanishes like ether.

Only one to go. The one I came here for.

I step to an unused area, its solitude making its lone tenant look like a pariah, I find my father's grave site. His headstone looks in no better shape than the others. I repeat the ground keeping process until my heart is happy with the accomplishment.

Without a word, I return to my car for a large cardboard box, the last of my father's things, and the reason for my visit. Jutting from one corner of the container is a broken-down fishing pole; the sections bound together with bread ties.

The box clatters as I put it down and seat myself in front of the marker where I can read it. I study the name on it as if it holds the answers to the universe. Perhaps it does.

"Hey, Dad." My jaw clenches after the words leave my mouth. I choke back the emotion. I sniffle and wipe a tear forming in the left corner of one eye. "Sorry. Allergies."

I'm lying to a corpse. What the hell is wrong with me?

"I found another box of your stuff the other day." I chuckle, the sound stopping dead before it morphs into something else. Composing myself, I lock eyes on the gravestone as if it could look back at me. "Can you believe that?" I read the date of his death, the mental math causing my lips to move. "Thirty years?"

I can't stop the head shake of disbelief. My shoulders droop as I let out a long sigh.

"Best get on with it, then."

I place a long-stemmed crimson rose on the marker. My hand dives into the box, retrieving a folded and mangled two-page letter I typed for this. Unfurling the papers, I clear my throat and begin to recite.

Dear Dad,

I've been hesitant to write this letter, despite wanting to do it for quite a while. I made every excuse I could to avoid this project, even halting my writing completely. I didn't know where to begin.

I wanted to be creative, making it a conversation between us. It's the writer in me, I suppose. I wasn't sure that I'd be able to do your voice justice since I can't remember it.

Then I found this little treasure trove of your things. That was when I knew it was time. I need this closure. Maybe you do too.

The ground below me lurches a bit. At least that's what it feels like. When it didn't happen again, I dismiss it as a trick of my imagination and continue reading aloud.

Today is Flag Day and the anniversary of your marriage to Mom. Father's Day is next weekend. I promised myself that I'd get this done before then so that I could read it to you. I hope I honor you the way God intended me to.

I know that I don't think about you as much as I should. I hope that doesn't hurt your feelings. I don't want to cause you pain in the afterlife.

You were a good father, a good provider, and a good role model for me. It may have taken me years to come to this enlightenment, or even admit it. That's my pride and stubbornness, rearing its ugly side. Let's admit I come by that honestly and move on, shall we?

I hope that I make you proud. I'm far from perfect, but I try to do the right thing every day, like you taught me. I know that there are things that I do that you might not have abided by. I won't make excuses. I don't know how you would have felt about your only son being gay.

After that admission, I rub my tattoos and touch my pierced ears. Once again, the ground shakes as if something rolls around beneath me. An explosion echoes in the distance.

You would have loved my husband. He's a bundle of energy who complements me. Mom and the family love and accept him as one of us. You would have, too. It may have taken a bit for you to get beyond the fact that I'm gay, or it may not have. There's always an adjustment period, I suppose. I can't recall where you stood on things like this. You'd think I'd remember your reactions with all the AIDS headlines in the news at the time.

The world seems to be unraveling all around us. I hate to think we are living in the "End Times," but the evidence is mounting. I hope I'm wrong. I don't fear death. I fear never being able to see my loved ones again. I don't fear hell or damnation. If God damned me from the beginning, then there's nothing I can do to prevent it.

Gunshots fire about a half mile away. No threat currently, so I continue, though my nerves are on high alert now.

If Heaven is a place without those I've lost over the years, then I'm not sure I want to go there, either. It won't be my paradise. What kind of heartless person could go into the afterlife and shrug their shoulders that someone they cared for won't be joining them?

I reach into the box and pull out the fishing pole: a Shakespeare spin-caster he once treasured. I could never get the hang of that type of reel. I always ended up with a tangle of line around the spool whenever I tried to cast it. I laugh at how "blue" my father's language would get when that happened.

I want to go fishing with you one last time. Even if I don't "hold my mouth right," and you out-fish me. I miss our days at the lake. The memories are bittersweet.

My hand finds the brass compass he left me. Popping open the latch, I watch the needle twirl around like the blades of a fan. My face scrunches at the sight.

It never did that when I used it for hiking.

I shrug it off as I place it on his gravestone.

I suppose I lost my way a bit after you passed; it took a while to realize how off-track I was.

Two of my biggest regrets in life center around you. They aren't your fault.

Mom and I sold the lake lot. As many memories as we made there, it wasn't getting used anymore. Practicality won over sentimentality. The solitude vaporized when a single family bought all the lots around it. They weren't bad people. I didn't enjoy having neighbors there. I sold it to them so that they could have the whole cul-de-sac. It only seemed right. Part of me would give the world to have it back, especially right now. Getting away from this madness may end up being necessary.

More gunshots ring around me; closer this time. Close enough that I hear people shouting and screaming.

"I'd better hurry up." I look around to place the direction of the commotion. "That action is getting way too close for comfort."

The other regret I have is far more important to me: the fact that I lied to you on your deathbed. You asked me point blank if I were gay. I fibbed right to your face about it. I knew even back then that it was a lie. I feared admitting the truth at the time. I was afraid of what you might think of me. Plus, with the audience I had, I couldn't bring out the truth I held inside. It took me another ten years to get comfortable enough to accept that part of myself. It was the one untruth I told you in my life that I still feel after all this time.

I can't recall much about our relationship beyond the arguments. I don't remember if you ever put me on your shoulders. I'm sure you did. I can't see an image of you in my mind past the one of you wasting away in your final hours. How heavy you must have felt. The hallucinations took your mind in those last days. We laughed at them as you suffered through the delusions.

All I could do was concentrate on how I felt. I was so selfish. I wanted out of there. I couldn't take it anymore. It was too much.

I can't stop the waterworks now. I'm not even sure that I want to. The country is tearing itself apart all around me in its Second Civil War. People are losing their lives over politics and extremists. It feels good to release. My tears water the green grass over my father's grave.

I'm going to leave now Dad. I may not be back again. My husband and I are boarding a plane tonight to leave the United States behind us, possibly for good. It's not what I want to do, but what I must. It's for survival. This country's become too hostile towards my type. It's gotten so bad that even families who protect us are being executed in the streets. I can't allow the rest of the family to suffer for our sake.

All in all, you were the best father anyone could have asked for. You weren't perfect. No one is. I'm not. You were the role model I needed, even if I didn't see it then. That is my final regret. I never showed you love or appreciation while you were alive. I turned and walked away as you lay dying from your illness. I should have been there for you. Please forgive me.

I love you.

Your son.

Another explosion shakes the ground. I fold the letter as small as I can, tucking it under my father's headstone. I remove the leather box of foreign coins he always kept on his dresser. Opening the latch, the treasure exposed to the smoky sky. I caress it one final time. Memories of the many excursions into the box come flooding back. I cherish the fantastic adventures my imagination would take me on when I explored the collection as a child.

"We need to go," exclaims my husband from the passenger side of the car. "Now!"

I nod, getting to my feet, my ancient knees popping like the gunshots around us. I hear more voices approaching. I wave my husband back into the car as I rush to the driver's side, my own pistol drawn.

If things take a turn before we speed off toward the airport, I'm prepared.

I'm not willing to die today. I'm not going to give up who I am. Not for the cultists tearing the world apart. Not for anyone.

I never see the hand reach up from below my father's marker and collect the letter.

IRON TO LEAD

The fatigue set in fast. It was the most noticeable of the symptoms. My life had become sleep, shower, work, eat, repeat. Then bathing became a chore, so I only did that every other day. Making dinner, even ordering take-out, became more of a bother than a necessity. My meals dwindled down from three squares to once per day, until I barely had the energy to lift a fork.

Looking in the mirror, my beard stubble grew only slightly slower than the bags under my eyes. Leering at the stranger in front of me, I splashed cold water on my face in a feeble attempt at energizing myself. The worry lines stayed. The puffiness clung to my visage like barnacles to a pier. My face sagged like a damp cloth on my skull.

One of my dad's favorite sayings was, "Did the iron in your blood turn into the lead in your ass?"

The sheer alchemy of this "dad-ism" always made me chuckle. I know that it was a commentary on how I was being lazy about something. I was also a kid back then, so the child in me loved the visual as well as the mild profanity of it. Now, it didn't seem quite so humorous.

The next day, my strength took a complete hiatus. Even untangling myself from the bed sheets winded me. Slinging my legs over the edge of the mattress, I felt for my slippers. Guiding my feet into them, my arms shook with effort as I stood up.

Maybe I should go to the doctor.

That little bit of whimsy was the last thing I recall before I woke up on the bedroom floor of my studio apartment. My eyes fluttered as strange people hovered over me. Every part of me felt leaden; unmovable. It was all I could do to open my eyelids.

"Who are you?" I recall asking one of them. Bastards mumbled their answer. One of the people – I think it was a woman with her hair pulled back into a tight bun – shone some sort of penlight into my eyes.

Rude.

The room became a blur of motion. I felt like I was being abducted. My body lifted into the air on its own. The ceiling morphed to bright light and blue sky, whirring by me at a panicked pace of its own accord. Then, the scenery above me changed to that of a large van or similar vehicle.

I don't know. My head couldn't make much sense of it. Tightness grew in my chest as my heart palpitated. A man plunged some sort of plastic mask over my nose and mouth.

Now I felt panic set in. Straining against the thing I was tied to was laughable. The vehicle lurched and a siren wailed in my ears. My fists clenched and released.

"Help," I muttered. In my foggy headedness, it felt like a scream. My eyes darted around, looking for anyone to hear my cries. "Help me."

One of them replied, but the world around me sounded as if I was being held underwater. Everything they said in response garbled like a child blowing through a straw into his milk.

One of the abductors pricked me.

By the time my head turned to protest, I felt too sleepy to fight for my life. Darkness swept over me like a weighted blanket.

When I awoke, every part of my body felt as if I'd been set in concrete. My limbs refused to move. Even my head couldn't shift upon my neck. A single light shone on me like a heathen sun, burning spots into my corneas.

Where am I?

A vain attempt at lifting my noggin only resulted in gravity reclaiming it like a prize. I squinted to shut out the invading light. Shadows contorted in my fuzzy periphery. I could scarcely make out the humanoid shapes. Their voices clicked and burbled, none of it making any sense. Whatever they were doing to me, they were in a hurry to get it done.

I've only seen lights that bright in one place in my life. I knew where I was now.

"Let me out of this warehouse." I could feel a rush of adrenaline hit me. I recognized this place. I worked here so many years ago. The job felt like a prison sentence then. Now, it also seemed to serve as my jail cell. My muscles finally responded. The restraints tightened under my indignation. "I'll beat the shit out of every one of you if you don't let me go."

The fire in my veins was short-lived. It was exhausting, and they had me at a disadvantage. My brain knotted with anger. I seethed at the figures as they paraded around me. My teeth gnashed; lips curled in a sneer of hate.

I heard Velcro tear on my dominant hand. The ties loosened. Now was my chance. I yanked my limb free and shoved one of the assailants away. I heard them stumble and clatter to the ground.

That was satisfying.

The dark blobs descended upon me. I pulled the tie off of my other arm and then swung. I hit one of the assailants, a crunching sound coming from the impact. Something wet spattered on my hand. God, it was triumphant.

Drool poured from my mouth. My feet were still confined. I pawed at the cuffs around my ankles. My fingers finally found the cuff, and one of my lower limbs sprung from its snare.

"Leave me alone," I growled, lashing out with all appendages while trying to regain my final bit of freedom.

Their mutterings were more acute as I fought them away. My ears rang and head ached. Standing on spaghetti legs, my arms tucked, I was ready to bring thunder down on anything daring too close. I was unable to keep my focus on anything; all images were still watery.

A black humanoid blob sprang at me. I lashed out but missed the mark. It entangled itself around my arm like a vine. Another of the things mimicked the act with my remaining arm. Struggling against my captors, I kicked at anything I could see. My toe found something metal, the vibrato of the impact shooting stars of pain into my head.

I felt another pinprick. The resistance left my body as fast as it had been born. The world spun back into darkness as my dead weight slipped from their grasp to the floor.

You win again.

Don't be here when I wake up.

Round two is coming.

PIGGYBACK

"Beware the Blood Rose!"

The sign didn't register. It intermingled with a slew of others decrying the attractions of the farm. Pulling up to the dusty parking lot, the place was hopping. The weathered red barn brimmed with patrons buying apple-based pastries and products. Baskets of all sizes were available for customers to go to the orchard and gather their own fruit. Children ran around petting and feeding various farm animals.

Pulling Kaleb from the car, Martin closed the door and tossed him high into the air, catching him on the return.

"Again, Daddy!" The toe-headed boy emitted a squeal of delight. His pale blue eyes glistened with glee as his father caught him in mid-air.

The man was well built and tanned from his work as a roofer. A few people in the park watched the two interact with smiles on their faces. The child was his spitting image, from his looks down to the tank tops and khaki cargo shorts they both wore. The only disparity was the wear and tear of age. As he caught Kaleb the last time, his shoulders gave a warning, causing him to wince. "Better not, kiddo." The disappointment on his boy's face broke his heart as he spun the child up and over his shoulders. "You're getting so big, and Daddy needs to save his energy."

Kaleb bent down and hugged his father's head. "Love you, Daddy."

Martin's heart thumped, his love for his son washing over him. "I love you more. Now, hold on tight."

Boyish giggles announced the start of their usual "Love you more" game as they galloped from the car.

"Let's go, daddy!" Kaleb bounced on Martin's shoulders. "I wanna pick apples!"

"You're the boss."

The late August cloudless sky offered no respite as the sun glinted off of the rust-patched tin roofs. Martin grabbed a bushel basket from the porch of the store, the thick wire handles bent from a season of heavy use. Setting the container down, he retrieved his ticket from the cashier. She was a young amputee. She sat in a wheelchair behind the ticket counter, tending to the business of the farm. Her skin had a greenish hue, thorns and leaves jutted from all parts of her body.

"Wow. Nice makeup. She's really into this business," Martin mused as he took his receipt from her.

"Beware the Blood Rose."

The sign, a much smaller version than the one by the road, plastered to the teller's glass with scotch tape at eye level. An elderly lady locked eyes with Martin, a quizzical look on her face. With a trembling finger, she pointed at the sign, tapping the glass. A muffled, "Be careful," came from within the booth. Then her hand went to her hip as if in pain.

Martin nodded as if he understood, shaking her off as if she were crazy once his back turned. Kaleb had climbed inside the basket, a huge grin on his precious face.

"Carry me!"

Martin shook his head and smiled. "I can't carry you in that basket. It's not built for little boys. It's made for fruit. Are you a fruit?" His grin widened, his eyes getting that ornery glint as he leaned down. "I know! Maybe you're a tickle fruit." His arms shot out toward his son, fingers waggling.

Kaleb squealed, the basket tipping on its side as he tried to escape. The boy rolled from the container, attempting to beat a hasty retreat. As he ran, he missed the first step off the porch.

"Kaleb, watch out." Martin's hand shot out. Time seemed to stand still as he watched Kaleb begin to plummet off the porch. In his fast-working mind, it almost seemed as if the roses had reached out for them both as he scooped Kaleb into his embrace. His arms and shoulders scraped against the thorny bushes lining the sides of the steps.

Kaleb let out a surprised screech as the bushes raked streaks into his little legs. After he was safe in his father's arms, the waterworks began.

Kaleb's pained wailing broke the father's heart. He stood the boy up, spinning him around and surveying the damage, ignoring his own injuries. Blood began trickling as Martin's ire boiled. "Who the hell thought it was a great idea to put roses next to stairs?"

The elderly woman in a light blue tee shirt and an apron rushed out to survey the damage. "Oh. The blood roses. Well, I did warn you." She glanced at Martin's arm with chagrin. "I'll get you cleaned up."

The father saw all the people staring at him and immediately blushed in shame at his commotion. "I'm sorry. I get hurt worse than this at work sometimes. A paper towel will do." He helped his son up, brushing off the backside of his shorts. He failed to see the minuscule thorns buried in the back of Kaleb's thighs. "Ready, champ?"

He thanked the aged woman as she handed him a napkin to blot the trailing blood. The boy grabbed his father's hand as they headed away from the store and into the vast orchard.

"Carry me, daddy!"

Martin began to pick him up, but his arm was being held back. The same lady from the store. She patted his wound.

"Are you sure you're both okay, son? You shouldn't trifle with blood roses. Nasty thorns. Nature's lessons." She leaned back, gaining a happy nod from her guest. "Did we get them all? We must be sure."

Martin nodded and gathered his child. She clapped a hand on his shoulder and whispered into his ear.

"Oh, let him walk. You'll spoil him." The woman patted him, a cheerful laugh under her breath.

The roofer felt his blood boil again, shooting the proprietor a stern look. "He's six. I'll raise my son how I want to." He shrugged her grasp with an indignant huff.

The lady's smile broadened, her voice singsong. "You shouldn't be so inseparable. A boy must learn to fall on his own and pick himself up. But," she muttered, "Who am I to tell you?" She chortled again, a hint of venom in her tone. "Enjoy the orchard. I hope it bears lots of fruit for you." She turned toward the storefront, her smile wilting away with her back to the pair. Her hand went instinctively to her hip as she winced, her face scrunched in pain. "Some people need to learn the hard way."

Martin grabbed his son's hand, leading him to the rows of trees in the distance. He kept his peripheral vision on the woman before she shut the door.

"Creepy-ass woman," he muttered.

"Creepy-ass woman," Kaleb parroted, much louder, looking up at his dad.

Martin knelt, grabbing his son by the shoulders and forced his son to face him. "I don't want you to use that language, okay? I shouldn't use it either." He could see tears well up in his son's eyes from the sudden shift in demeanor.

"It's not nice words?" Kaleb's bottom lip trembled.

The father smiled, pulling his son in for a tight hug. "That's right."

Kaleb yammered on while they strolled. Listening to his son's wonder and amazement filled Martin's heart even more. Soon, their trifle with the rose bush was forgotten.

Swallowtail butterflies flitted about, tasting the rotting fruit on the ground. The flies were thicker here, but they stuck to the bad apples carpeting the grass. Neat rows of pruned trees spanned out in front of them. Clusters of ripening apples weighed down the branches, ripe for picking. The sharp pang of decaying produce filled the light breeze. Cicadas screamed their ode to the end of summer. Kaleb marveled at the trees, only having ever eaten apples from a grocery store. A handful of fruit rolled around in their basket while Martin explained how to find one that was ripe.

"There's one, daddy. I'll climb up and get it."

The father followed his son's finger to the top of the eight-foot-tall tree. Near the crown was the brightest red ball all alone. "Yeah. You're not about to go up there. It's pretty high up." Then he got an idea. "Hang on, buddy. I'll help you get it." Reaching down, he picked Kaleb up and set him on his shoulders.

"Ow!" They both yowled in unison.

Pinpricks shot sharp pains into Martin's shoulders.

"My legs are burning. Make it stop, daddy." Kaleb tried to kick his feet but found them unmovable. He screeched in agony as thorny vines whipped between the pair. They sewed themselves into father and son, stitching the two together like a suit.

Martin's eyes widened as his son's legs pulled against him. The vines threaded between his ribs and collar bones. They twined around the boy's muscles. Blood poured from their wounds, the tendrils tailoring them into one.

White-hot fever erupted between their bodies. Man and boy both wailed in agony as onlookers gawped in shock. Cries echoed across the field of trees.

The elder shopkeeper stepped out onto the sun porch, wiping her hands on her apron. She glowered towards the ruckus in the distance. Her granddaughter struggled to see over the matriarch in an attempt to figure out what was going on. The old woman shook her head and glanced at the dew-glistening blood rose. "Some people don't listen." She disappeared back into the store without a second look.

Back in the orchard, Martin had withered to his knees. He balanced a sobbing and snotty Kaleb atop his broad shoulders. The initial wave of pain had finally subsided, leaving them exhausted and breathless. People gathered around them in wonder and horror. Voices buzzed like insects in a chorus of shock. Kaleb wilted over his father's head, his arms dangling.

The sudden shift of weight forward jerked Martin back to attention. His hands shot to his offspring in worry.

"Kaleb! Kaleb!" Tugging at his child, he tried to dismount the boy, unable to budge him.

Kaleb's clothes had fallen away; only the outlines of his legs showed where their skin touched. Little feet and toes hovered over Martin's nipples like perverse eyelashes. The dad looked around at the audience, some of them snapping pictures and video with their phones.

"Help us, you goddamn idiots! Stop gawking and call 9-1-1."

He pawed at his son trying anything to get him to stir, but the boy had passed out. Kaleb's breath rasped in his ear, sending waves of chills down his spine. Standing on shaky legs, Martin righted himself. Kaleb lolled to one side, nearly tipping them both to the ground. Martin's neck and shoulders ached. He turned to the retreating crowd, a pleading hand extended. His breath caught in his throat.

"Is my boy okay? Please. Anyone. Tell me my son is okay."

A dark-haired woman in a wide-brimmed hat set down her basket of fruit and approached, fearful. She flinched as Martin turned to her before reaching up to the boy. She felt the child's neck.

"He has a pulse, but it's weak. He's in shock."

Her touch went to the seam of their conjoined bodies. The flesh blended to the point where it was difficult to tell where one stopped and the other started. Small branches began to grow from random parts of Kaleb's body. Thorns spiked through his skin. The child's deep summer tan shifted to a greener color. Martin felt his knees buckle again, as his son's dead weight listed to the side. The woman assisted him back to the ground.

"Easy. Easy. You should sit until help arrives." Her eyes watered over as she guided the pair to a lower center of gravity. Her hand went to the child's face. Martin felt the thoughtful caress as if it were on his own cheek. His heart thudded. Kaleb stirred.

"What's going on?" The father tried to hide the crackling in his voice. His pleading eyes met the only person who bothered to help them. "Why is this happening?"

The pale, porcelain-skinned lady only shook her head, offering no explanation. Her touch comforted him, even in her silence.

"My name is Brenda," she soothed, as if that were the answer to his questions. "We'll get you through this. Whatever it is."

"I told you. It's a lesson," offered an aged voice behind her, causing the lady to start. It was the shopkeeper. The old woman sneered at the melded father and son, the crowd parting to allow her entrance. "They have to learn it on their own."

"You!" Martin attempted to stand, but Brenda held him down. "Let me up. Let me at that bitch. She did this to us."

"Oh, no sir," the gray-haired and wrinkled woman assured him. "You did it to yourselves. I tried to warn you."

She untied her apron.

"Sometimes…" She began to lift her sun dress to one side. The crowd gasped, unsure of what to expect. "We old folk speak from experience." Around her hip was the outline of a pair of small legs with nothing attached to them. They looked as aged as she was, yet rotten, cancerous, swollen. Dying brown stems poked outward all around the lump. After the onlookers got their eyeful, she dropped her clothes back into place. "Now the blood rose made you as one. As it had my granddaughter and I."

"What's going on, Gramma?" The audience gave a wider berth, allowing the greenish young girl in a wheelchair into view. Her legs were missing, removed at mid-thigh. She shifted her head all around to get a good look.

Wheeling her way to the front, her soft eyes rained hope upon the father and son as Martin gaped at her in disbelief. She shone a knowing smile.

"It'll be okay." In the distance, sirens wailed their approach. The girl peered in the direction of the nearing medics. "It won't be easy, but everything will be alright."

DO WHAT I MUST

Things started out a bit rough when my flight crashes on this island. To think that I bitched about being in the tail end of the plane. In retrospect, the smell from the bathroom was worth it, even on a flight across the Pacific. If I ever see civilization again, I will only fly if I have another middle seat between two passengers. I'm convinced that's how I survived the crash.

The trees sway in a salty night sea breeze. It's hypnotic. And the stars? I had no idea so many were out there. Even in a planetarium, I'd never seen so many. Magical. The sides of my leathery shelter ruffle in tune with the fronds of the looming palms. A coconut thumps against the tent, rolling harmlessly to the side of the structure.

"Missed, bitch," I tease the fates, chuckling to myself.

I am the only survivor from my section of the plane. Hell, for the longest time, until the others find me, I thought I was the only one. I did what I could to get by. The remnants of my section of the plane offer a bit of shelter, but the elements still get to me. As I scavenge the wreckage, I find a big Bowie knife from the trail of luggage scattered everywhere. It makes things   so   much   easier.

First, I skin the bodies around me, drying their hides in the sun. Human skin is waterproof. Did you know that? The passengers who sat next to me taste like pork chops when roasted over an open fire. So juicy and marbled.

I loathe it when the others find me. An old man, two injured women, and a kid. My solitude is wrecked. Worse, they treat me like I'm an animal because I know how to survive. Oh sure, they are all about sharing my home with me. Most of them don't ask where I got the meat. The kid is inquisitive. I told him that it was long pig. That was a trick my own father would use as a kid to get me to try different meats. The boy doesn't get the joke, even as he chews. It's the geezer that puts the pieces together. I think it's the tattoo that gives it away. Not on me; on my tarp.

Everyone else is desperate to get back home. Not me. They start signal fires. At night, I sneak over and put them out. To me, this desolation isn't a curse. It's a blessing.

The old man has to be the first to go. Besides, the rest of the meat is going bad, and I can feel him plotting against me.

You can't imagine the knife's satisfying sound as I plunge it into the top of his skull. It is almost musical. His flesh isn't good for much, but his pelt stretches nicely. I did this away from the women and the boy. The brunette will die soon. The bone jutting from her left leg already smells like almonds. She is running a fever and muttering. Dammit. That means her meat won't be edible.

The kid is working my nerves the most, though. His near-constant bawling and whimpering makes me impatient. If I wanted to hear spoiled brats wail like this, I'd have stayed on land and gone to the nearest department store. As much as it bothers me, I know he has to be last. No one to get all indignant when I slaughter him.

Finally, the woman with the broken leg passes. We bury her whole. What a waste. As we mourn at her graveside, I wait for the boy to go off and play. That's when I slit the other woman's throat. I'm hungry, and she is fresh meat. She'll last the boy and I a few days before it would be time to move on.

But what should I do with him?

I've heard that the younger flesh is, the better it tastes.

I should teach him how to whittle as my father had taught me.

My stomach growls at me.

Fine.

I suppose the decision is made.

I close my eyes, thinking about that final hunt. He doesn't go easily. I'll hand it to him; his survival instincts may rival my own. He looks like a piglet on a spit over the fire. Some of the meat I dry from his corpse will last a little while.

I'm so glad that I escaped that institution before the flight. They'll never find me here.

LIKE FATHER, LIKE SON

"You're not holding your mouth right."

As a kid, my father would out-fish me. I'd get annoyed, even upset. It seemed like he could cast anywhere and catch a fish. My God, how I envied, even hated his skill. Hell, when I'd give up and go swimming, he'd cast right next to me and still sink a hook. He was always careful enough not to get too close, or he'd get a real catch. Still, he'd reel in a bluegill or something for me to fillet later.

Ugh. I always regretted the day he taught me to clean the meat off a fish. They were slimy, stinky, and gross. They sure tasted good when he or Mom cooked them, though.

Those were the good old days. Then, it was sport and a good meal. We always ate what we caught. Now, it's a necessary thing. I catch the fish, cut the useful parts away, and use the carcasses for fertilizer. Sometimes the woodland critters would get into them and take what they wanted. I let them. There was plenty to go around.

I wished that my father was more of a hunter when he was alive. I'm getting burned out on fish dinners. I haven't the slightest idea of how to skin anything else. I suppose I could be proactive and teach myself, but I'm surviving. That's good enough.

He used to bring me here to get away from the noise of the city. Back then, it was more for his sake than mine. I was young and easily bored. That's why he kept me busy with the upkeep of this place as he watched on, criticizing the minutiae of my tasks.

I appreciated the serenity. The calls of the whippoorwill or an owl at night. The churring of the insects screaming their serenade of madness at the summer wind. The leaves of the trees rustle in a nice low breeze. I loved it all.

It was off the grid, and off the map. Our little oasis. Out here, there was no one to bother me. The world could turn upside-down all it wanted to. Very few knew about this place, most of them residents who kept to themselves as well, especially now.

I shoveled another heaping of dirt onto the fresh hole. "You have to dig them deep," he'd say, "to keep others from nosing about." He taught me that for burying anything from our fish remnants to our poop.

On this little tract of land, we buried many family pets. Most of them had no idea that this place even existed. They'd never been here in their short little lives. It was one place where they could still be a part of us, even after they had passed. I'd mark their graves with a stone, or a homemade cross, and even write their names on it. Time always took its toll. It would rot away the wooden markers or wash away the hand-scrawled name. All that was left would be the memory of where they had been put to rest.

Another spade of dirt flew into the gorge I had dug. The sound of it hitting the canvas was satisfying.

The air that billowed from within the package wasn't as appealing.

Everything goes back to nature. Our pets, our catch, even my father did when we buried him here. It all returns to dust. I will, too, I'm sure, at the right time. Everything eats. Everything defecates. Everything dies. The only real constant is that the world keeps spinning. It goes on. Everyone wants to leave a mark, yet, when it's all boiled down to the vastness of the universe, no one does.

It's amazing how much contemplation happened as I packed this hole. The stench of the earth filled my nostrils, dominating the campfire burning itself out.

I'm now older than he was when I was born, this toil taking the wind from my sails. If it weren't for the smell, I'd be in no hurry. I needed to get enough of the hole filled so that I no longer have that sickly sweet odor of decay invading my mind. Once I was done and the sun came up, I could rest.

Fulfilling my father's wishes proved to be a far more monumental task than I thought. He wanted us, his family, buried alongside him. I looked over to his grave. Time washed the dirt mound level to the surroundings long ago. Now, wildflowers bloomed all around and atop it. He would have approved. Mom, however, had her own plans. She wanted her ashes spread to the many places that made her happy. Her last will and testament was far less strenuous to make true. A little bit of her was here, on top of her husband. Some of her on the shore of the Gulf of Mexico. Some of her in California, where she made many memories.

Sweat beaded on my brow, and my heart palpitated from the strain. The cool night air helped, but this is exercise that I'm unused to. Finally, a good layer accumulated on top of the body within the ground. I tossed in the remnants of today's catch, wrapped in newspaper.

Why dig two holes?

I got a second wind. Scoop after scoop of dirt returned to the hollow I pulled it from. The odor lingered for a bit more, getting fainter with each inch.

Mosquitoes buzzed around my ears, the one place I failed to get any kind of deterrent slathered onto my skin. Their little wings droned before they landed to attempt a feast on my blood. I swatted them, smashing the pests flat.

The more this burrow refilled, the quicker my shoveling got. It was a sense of accomplishment. It became a reward for a job well done once the final bit of sod and gravel were placed at the apex of the former crater.

I sat and unwound by the dying embers of the fire, contemplating skewering a marshmallow and bringing it to a proper char. I twisted the top off ice-cold water and chugged it like beer at a frat party. Tossing the empty bottle onto the fire, I watched the black smoke dance into the sky as the remaining droplets sizzled. The plastic curled into a black blob, evaporating away as well.

I don't know whether my husband wanted to be buried here or not. I suppose I should have asked him first. Guess it's too late to worry about it now. I may be joining him soon.

I do love the tranquility of these woods. The birds don't care about what I've finished doing. They want to sing to the night. Now, I can listen. The insects scrape their wings together to find a mate.

Mine will forever be here with me.

FATHER FIGURE

My father instilled in me a love for camping. He was an outdoorsman, and he gave me a greater love of nature. As an older parent - he was fifty years old when I was born - He didn't get to do many of the things he would have liked. He retired from his job around the same time I entered into puberty; not a great mix for the summer months at the time. The moments we'd spent together in those months formed the uneasy relationship we had.

It's funny how memories like this pop up during times of distress. I sat on the rocky formation. Large, sticky snowflakes pattered my face before melting. I chopped several branches into small tent stakes for an emergency shelter. I should have listened to my friends when they warned me against hiking in the mountains. They told me that the weather had a habit of changing on a whim around where I wanted to go. I'm an experienced hiker, but a tourist to this part of Colorado.

Two things my dad could never work out of me are my stubbornness and my know-it-all attitude. They are also two things I inherited from him.

I had bells on my shoelaces to prevent surprising wildlife. My backpack had warmer clothes for the shift in temperature, and plenty of water and food for a day's hike. I'd be fine.

Famous last words. And they very well might be mine.

I tied a small canvas tarp and stretched it over a low-hanging branch. It looked like a decent shelter. It acted more like a wind tunnel, the snow drifting inside as if invited in for cookies.

An experienced hiker, my ass.

I shivered in my hooded jacket, holding my phone up, cursing at the lack of service. The last text message I got was over a mile below on a thin switch-backed trail. The snow had already covered the path I used to get up here. Between the pine needles on the ground and the lichen on the rocks, finding my own path would be treacherous. One slip and gravity would take it from there. I may have no choice. I can't start a fire. The smallest blaze could become a full-scale forest fire within seconds. I wasn't quite at the top of the tree line, but the vegetation was much thinner here, as was the air.

Clouds roiled both above and below me, only the peaks of the other mountaintops visible. It must have been my mind losing its grip when I saw the silhouette of a man motioning for me. I shouted at him for help, but he gestured for me to follow, never speaking a word. I couldn't shake the feeling of familiarity. I never saw more than a blurry outline; a spectral shadow guiding me.

The snow began blowing sideways, the dark figure obscured by drifting white. The elements did their best to separate us. No matter how many times I called to the specter, it remained at the same distance from me like a mirage. I never gained on it, and it never approached me.

My foot slipped on a snow-covered rock, and down I went. I felt the sound as much as I heard it. Pair that with the stars I saw when my head hit the ground, and I knew I must have cracked my noggin. Red hot pain flared from my knee and my head, competing for attention. Bleary-eyed, I swallowed back the overwhelming desire to give up. The shadowy figure stopped, still at a distance.

"Get up, son."

The speech boomed like thunder in my head, but my focus couldn't place the source of the familiar voice.

"Move. Now!"

I heard a crack in the canopy of pine trees above me. I rolled out of the way as a dead branch speared the earth where I had been. Eyes wide in shock, my heart thumped as I continued leaking blood from the gash in my scalp. The limb vibrated from the impact, billowing a cloud of snow into the frigid air, and then crashed to the ground.

As I stood on uneasy legs, I looked at the fallen branch, then at the shimmering figure. It seemed to leer at me, though it was difficult to tell. Only pinpricks of light shone where its eyes should be. The ghost began beckoning me closer with a wave.

"Do you want me to follow you?" I shouted through the wailing wind.

The figure appeared to nod, still waving me on. An arctic blast cut through my meager coat, chills dancing on my skin. Flurries plopped into my eyes, obscuring my vision even more as they melted.

"I can't see the path."

The specter continued, unrelenting, guiding me through the uneven terrain. The cloud cover obscured what was below; the howling wind and snow pelted me from above. Still, the shadow remained at a distance, coaxing me forward.

I could make out a narrow, stony trail, the lines blurred by the storm. Rocks loosened under my feet, falling into oblivion. My shoulder bumped into the mountainside, and I almost spun to my death alongside the gravel. My injured knee refused my weight under the steadiest ground. Now, it protested with flares of agony and an unsure gait.

"Wait," I plead with the ghost. "I still... I can't see."

"Stop, son."

I finally placed the voice reverberating in my skull. It was my father's. It had to be. Gone for over thirty years since my childhood, my mind struggled for memories.

Was that what he sounded like? I couldn't recall. Cocking my head to the side, I lifted my foot.

"No. Not another step."

The apparition before me urged me on, yet that familiar tone caused me to freeze in place.

Finally, the wind ceased for a few precious seconds of relief. I could still see the shadow motioning me to follow as the air cleared. My eyes widened at the yawning abyss only a single stride away from the tip of the slag I was on. I thumped against the craggy mountain, my heart drumming in my ribcage at the close call.

Still, the dark creature tempted me forward. Instead, I side-shuffled my way back to solid land. My pulse thrummed in my head and knee. As I sat, that surgical breeze cut into me with its icy knives. Puffs of white blew and floated around me, yet there the thing stood, waiting. Its unblinking gaze never faltered.

"Who are you?" I growled at the spirit. "What are you?"

I looked on in terror as the wraith's face split into a rictus grin, the blowing flakes wafting through its smile. The sight chilled my blood.

"Stay put," uttered the disembodied voice. "The storm will clear."

Yet the presence before me continued to call me to action.

I snatched a fistful of the falling powder, tossing it at the vile vision. "Go to hell. Whatever you are." I pulled my knees to my chest and tucked my head between them to shelter my face from the arctic bluster. Dampness soaked my legs now, this time from my falling tears. I wailed back at the wind, muffled through my limbs.

"I'm going to die here, aren't I?"

"Stay strong."

Once again, the voice I heard contradicted the phantasm before me. It beckoned to me with a curling finger as it swayed in a breeze that didn't match the wind of the storm. Its eyes began to glow red, causing my stomach to drop. Gazing upon it brought a chill rivaling the storm, yet I couldn't break the trance it had on me.

It continued to wave me forward. Before I knew it, I was standing, eye contact unbroken. Losing control of my feet, I stepped toward the apparition, unable to stop myself.

I felt resistance on my shoulders, something, or someone, tugging me away. It held the top part of me back, despite my lower half's continued momentum.

The earth slipped beneath me, sending me back down to the ground. Stars shot across my vision, flares of agony down my spine. A coppery taste filled my mouth. My eyes watered. Every bit of air rushed from my lungs in a tremendous burst.

As the air seemed to pulse around me in tune with my heartbeat, I lay still, recovering. I coughed, releasing a glob that spattered the white snow with crimson droplets. I reached inside my mouth, feeling a throbbing in my teeth. The jarring had caused a crown to free itself. I pulled it loose with a sickening crunch.

I found myself unable to take deep breaths without my lungs aching. The cold, cutting air of the tempest tore at my desire to live.

I wanted to give up.

The sky finished pissing frozen hell on me. The clouds seemed to mock me, departing as suddenly as they had appeared. A sunbeam shone, warming my face with what felt like a final taunt.

"Fuck you."

My body jerked backward. All color washed from my face as I leered, wide-eyed, over my shoulder. The creature had me by my left ankle, dragging me toward the precipice. It smiled; a smoky, horrific grin, highlighted by the crimson eyes.

"Die," it growled. "Your soul is mine."

I kicked at it with my free foot. It passed through, the damnable abomination never losing its grasp.

"Fight, son," the paternal voice instructed. "If you don't finish it, it will never leave you alone."

"How?" I screamed, continuing my attempted assault on the wisp that ensnared me. "How do I fight it?"

"Die," the thing repeated, yanking me closer still. The cushion of snow wasn't enough to prevent the craggy rocks from tearing at my body.

My legs dangled in the air. I could feel gravity's embrace begin to pull me over the edge. I clawed for purchase against the sensation of sliding down to my doom. It yanked once more. I grasped at a root buried beneath the new blanket of white. My lungs ached as I screamed from the strain, my heart palpitating.

Kick. Nothing.

"Die."

"Eat shit," I defied.

"Son," my father's voice whispered, "You have to want to live." He paused. "Live for yourself. For your family. For your friends. Live for me."

I felt his reassuring touch return my strength to me. One of the branches I had sharpened to a point flew within my grasp. Using the point to dig into the cracks of the granite, I pumped my feet as I pulled myself completely onto land. The grotesque lost its grip. I was free.

I chuckled at the thing as it grimaced back. It roared at me. I gave it the New York salute. In one final act of defiance, I flung the pointed stick at the ghost like a spear. The thing's final howl would be its last as it dissipated like a dream.

"You can't have me." I chortled; the weight of the creature's haunting on me lifting like storm clouds. I sat on the ground, my arms once again wrapped around my knees. The light laughter continued, despite the dull ache in my chest. "Nope. Not yet."

I meditated there for a while as the sun melted the snow. Every part of my body was in agony, but my spirit felt lighter. I descended the path, collapsing as I returned to the trailhead. The demon of depression clawing at me had left me exhausted.

After I recovered from my sojourn, the world felt more welcoming. My body healed alongside my mind. I felt gratitude for those around me. A journey of self-indulgence became transformative. The world was a brighter place with me in it. I wouldn't have appreciated that if I'd let the darkness inside of me win that day.

Sure, the specter may revisit me at some point. It may even win the next time. For now, I'll live.

PIERCINGS

When I was a kid, my father showed me how to whittle a point on a stick. Little did I know, it was a survival skill that I'd use. I suppose most people wouldn't think what I do to myself as a form of "survival," but it is.

He also advised me that if I were ever to come home with a piercing, he'd rip it out of me. "Not in my house." That was his mantra about body modifications of any kind.

Out of respect or fear, I kept my word that I wouldn't do things like that until I was grown. When I finally left home, they became a symbol of my identity. It was a middle finger to the near-puritanical strictness I had grown up with.

I digress.

You might wonder why this is "survival" in my mind. It's my way of "cutting," I suppose, my mental anxiety given a physical representation.

Looking down at my body, I glossed over the dried or dripping blood. The pain caused by the insertion of the sharpened sticks into various parts of my body were now numbed by time. The focal points of the wooden intruders turned red, angry, and swollen.

I had piercings long before this, done by experts. I also had tattoos; the pictographs on my skin now distorted by the inserts beneath them. They say that tattoos and piercings can be addictive. I should have listened.

It started with smaller items like toothpicks and bamboo kabob skewers. The pain was exquisite. The movement of my clothes reminded me of their presence with each step of my feet or sway of my arms. Eventually, it wasn't enough. The agony would subside. Time to find another spot to drill a spike into.

They always had to be wood. Metal didn't do it. I don't know if it was the sharpness of the tips of the needles and gauges or if it was the unnatural feel of the material. Only plant-based sticks felt right. My brain couldn't identify with the smoothness and flawlessness of anything metallic. Only the coarseness of slivers entering my body felt correct.

The pain from the objects pricking through me was the only thing that silenced the voices in my head. Keeping a proper level of agony prevented the thoughts rattling between my ears from telling me to hurt people I love, or even strangers. I wouldn't feel compelled to stab the guy in the store carrying on a loud one-sided conversation in the aisles. I wouldn't suffer from the urge to stuff a crying infant back into its mother's body.

Now I've run out of options. Nothing is working. The swish of clothes no longer quieted my mind like white noise against its heathen desires. No. It wasn't about my survival. It was about the survival of others.

I volunteered at the twenty-story-high war memorial several years ago. I was a security guard there. Not that the place needed it. A few rambunctious teens. Emotional elders weeping at a dead relative's nameplate. The occasional heatstroke victim, or other medical emergency. Nothing too exciting or strenuous, but it gave me access to parts that the public didn't have; the part that I needed.

Below me is the dead tree I had chopped down, the fine point of its trunk jutting from the ground. Its allure called to me. One final piercing. A shiver danced over my body as I studied the trunk from this high angle. I fibbed to the curator of the museum. I had plans to make it into something artistic. It was only a partial lie, playing the long game leading to this very moment.

The wind caressed my naked body. The other patrons were long gone. It was peaceful up here, even with the cooing of the pigeons.

Damned shit-demons.

Studying myself, I couldn't stop the slight chuckle that escaped me. I looked like I got into a fight at a kabob competition. I resembled a porcupine. Or one of those leather-clad things from that horror movie everyone loved so much. Looking over the ledge, the ground seemed so far away. The world swam for a few seconds as I stared down from the dizzying height.

I climbed the wall, stepping over the chain-link fence. The razor wire curling around the top graced my skin with fresh cuts. All the fencing was installed to prevent people like me from doing this very thing. Still, it's not enough to prevent my mission.

It won't matter if I got the math wrong or didn't calculate for the wind. Another giggle escapes me as I recall something I overheard my father say once. We were watching a Charles Bronson or Clint Eastwood movie - they were his favorite actors.

"It's not the fall that killed him," my dad would muse after a bad guy plummeted from his perch, a sly smirk on a corner of his mouth. "It's the sudden stop."

Guess we'll find out, old man.

I look behind me as I position myself. If I live, the pain will be brutal enough to shut out the voices for a good long time. If I miss, even the rain-softened ground won't be forgiving enough, and I'll be unable to move on my own for the rest of my life.

At least no one else will get hurt.

Taking a deep breath, I relaxed and let go. Time froze, tendering me weightless, blissful, before gravity caressed me. The rush silenced my crowded thoughts for a few lovely, heavenly seconds.

Just one final piercing.

BEDSIDE REGRET

My heart thumped in my chest, the lump in my throat growing. I cracked the door to my parents' bedroom, peering through the opening. My mother was holding my father's hand. A steady stream of tears rolled down her cheeks.

She looked up at me as I emerged from the other side of the portal. "Come over here. He wants to see you."

My eldest sister was in from Michigan; a welcome guest, helping my mom during these final days. She sat at the foot of the bed, rubbing my mother's back and my father's legs at the same time.

I swallowed my own waterworks. Clearing my gullet, I approached with the uncertainty of a mouse nearing a trap. Nothing in my teenage wisdom could prepare me for this moment. Everything within me wanted to scream and run away. His eyes weren't fixated on anything. He lay there in bed, his gaze never leaving the ceiling, drool dripping from his slacked mouth. Mom would dab at it with a tissue to prevent his pillow from getting soaked.

I could hear mumbles exiting his scratchy throat, most of them whispered, incoherent. "No. I haven't counted my till yet. Why?" I stifled a laugh as my mom got up to let me have her seat right next to him. He hadn't worked in a convenience store in decades. This had been a theme for his hallucinations. I was getting regaled with stories each day after high school. They had spoken of it so comically that I couldn't help but chuckle.

They both joined me in a good snort. It might have been disrespectful had others been there. Under the circumstances, we took our laughter wherever we could get it in the circumstance. It was a welcome, albeit nervous, tension release.

I put my weight on the edge of the bed to prevent sitting on him. Gathering his hand and patting it, I watched him lift his head to see why the caress had changed. His weak smile beamed at me before his gaze returned upwards.

"There he is," he smiled weakly, taking a deep, raspy breath, "my handsome boy. I hope you know how much I love you."

The dam broke and my shoulders heaved as a waterfall formed on my cheeks. A fistful of fresh tissue was thrust in front of my face. I looked up, my vision watery, thanking my mom as I used them. She stroked my shoulder and left the room. I could still feel my sister rubbing my back and hear her reassuring me from behind. I jumped a little from her caress, having forgotten her presence.

"I love you too, Dad," I finally managed to squeak out - a brief interlude in the deluge of emotion.

"Okay. I'll ask." I tilted my head as my father strained to lift his from the pillow again to look at me.

He studied me as if unsure of how to get the information his heart desired.

"Ask what, Dad?" I tried to provoke whatever conversation haunted him.

"Son?" It wasn't a question of uncertainty or identification. He still stared at me as if deciding whether this was something that he wanted to know the answer to. "Are you gay?"

My mind blanked. I could feel the sweat begin to pour in tides that matched my tears. I'm certain that my heart stopped completely, if only to pause from shock. Words caught like glass in my throat.

"I..." I stammered, still reeling. "I don't know if you should ask me that."

"You haven't answered me." I sensed a bit of rage in his tone. The man whose favorite television characters were rough, tough males, demanded satisfaction. He wanted to know if his youngest child, his only son, would ever be like the actors he adored.

My face flushing and my lips trembling; I wiped my hands on my jeans before grasping his again. I searched his eyes for what I thought he might want to hear. They returned only questions marks hanging by a thread to his conscious mind.

To this day, my fear of being different is one of my life's largest regrets. I lied to my father as he lay preparing to meet his maker.

I denied the accusation. I believed it was what he wanted to hear; what I wanted to hear. He stared at me for a while, appearing to absorb my reply. His other quaking arm reached across and patted my hand.

"I'm tired," he informed the room, his arms and head going to limp position. "I need my sleep now." He closed his eyes to sleep for a bit. I recognized that glint of disbelief. It was the same one that was a precursor to trouble as a kid when something around the house got broken.

My sister placed her hand on my shoulder and escorted me out. "Let's let him be for now." The years of smoking had left her voice raspy and deep.

I walked from the room, my gaze at my father unbroken the entire time. My knees crumbled beneath me as we closed the door behind us. Collapsing to the floor, I knew what I had done.

Kneeling in a growing puddle of my own tears, I became acutely aware. It wasn't the missed opportunity; it was the sheer terror that I had lied. All for my own selfishness. All for my need for self-preservation. I lied to the man who had raised me. I lied to him and now it couldn't get taken back. The weight of it was phenomenal.

On my hands and knees, my back and shoulders lurched in heaving sobs. My mother and sister each tried to get me to my feet, but I shrugged them off. I needed to take in what had transpired on my own. I feared that it would be the last thing I would ever say to my "old man."

It was.

****

Now I'm lying here, thirty years in the future, twenty of it spent with the same loving man by my side. That single event has haunted me since. Before now, it had been a figurative haunting: the kind that eats at your spirit.

Tonight, on the anniversary of his death, I find myself paralyzed by fear as a specter moans my name. The tone in his voice, his outstretched hands, make him seem as if he's prowling. He's hunting for me. His outline is angular and abstract, his movements jerky and sudden. Still, I know it's him in my soul. I can feel it. It echoes the memory of his voice as he calls my name in the darkness of the room, searching. The terror is as transparent as the spectral spectacles it wears around its nose. What little moonlight leaks into the room glints off them. The glasses are the most prominent of the ghastly visitor's features. There are no eyes behind them.

My husband lies next to me, snoring away as I fret about this unholy visitor. I reach over to awaken him. He's deep in the embrace of the sandman.

My lizard brain goes right back into self-preservation mode. My heart tries to escape my rib cage as the damnable thing draws nearer. Tingles invade my tightening chest and one of my arms go completely numb. I squint my eyes shut, muttering prayers that the thing will pass me by.

One of my father's favorite quotes to keep my rebellious teen brain in line was that he'd put "the fear of God in me."

He's doing that now.

Sweat drenches my pillow. Terror locks every joint in my body. I am unable to move, unable to speak. I can no longer wake my husband from his slumber to know if he also sees my visitor. I can feel my pulse in my ears as my lungs lurch for air. A scream freezes in my throat.

The wraith continues to call my name, its arms flowing wisps of smoke as they blindly search. A deep, painful chill, like frostbite, climbs my legs as the ghost passes through the foot of the bed.

My mind frees my muscles at last, allowing me to escape the chilling grasp of the specter. I flop to the floor beside my bed, my partner still oblivious in his rest. He shivers a bit, adjusting the covers of his nightly cocoon. The nightmare continues to wail my name into the night.

Is this truly my father visiting me?

My thoughts scramble in the dead of the night as I spring to my feet. His voice sounds pained, tormented. He floats there by my loving spouse, seeming to twist his head back and forth in curiosity. My husband rolls onto his back, smacking dry, sleepy lips. The shadow continues to gauge interest.

I see black tendrils touch my love's bearded face. The chill sends a shudder down his spine that causes his face to furrow. He shivers beneath the bed sheets.

"Why?"

The agony in the visitor's inflection shatters my heart. I fall to my knees, my mind a whirlwind of hopeless possibilities. Hearing that single word come from something, at least pretending, to be my father. It forces a choice at the crux of a dark road in my brain.

"Because that's who I love," I whisper into the quiet night.

The thing examining my better half shifts its attention to my direction. It still doesn't see me, but now it knows my location.

I need to lure it away from him.

"Why?" it repeats, its movements becoming twitchy and disjointed. The atmosphere feels heavier, thicker.

I shuffle backward, doing what I can to keep the thing's attention on me. Retreating from the bed in this crowded and cluttered room, I stumble over shoes jutting from under the bed in my attempt to escape.

"Why?" This time, it seems to growl the question, more of a threat than an inquisition. The shadowy figure seems to slip through the space between us in an instant.

The coldness descends upon me, unrelenting in its fury. I drop to all fours again, feeling the thing twine itself around my very spirit. As its grasp reaches my heart, I know its true intentions.

And I weep.

"I..." I stammered through the deep sorrow in my soul. "I'm sorry that I lied to you, Dad. I had no idea how you would feel."

It grasps me, raising me up from the ground. As I'm back to standing upright, I experience a new, warmer sensation. Tears stream down my face as I look at the phantom of the man I once knew. Shame weighs heavy on me until I finally lock onto his eyes, the ones that were missing before.

"You're my son," the spirit comforted, "I could never not love you. Why didn't you trust me enough to tell me the truth?"

I begin to answer, leaning into his barrel-like corporeal chest instead. Despite its ethereal appearance, it felt solid and right. "I was so scared. I was young. I was unsure, even though I knew what I liked." I continued after a deep sigh, "I didn't want to be a disappointment. Not to you. Not to Mom. Not to anyone."

"You would have been safe..."

"I didn't know that," I snapped at the poltergeist. "We lived in a small town. I heard horror stories. Guys thought it was okay, even a triumph, to beat the crap out of guys like me. Even your reactions to the news when gays lay dying of AIDS made me second-guess where you stood."

Pausing to regain a bit of composure, I slide down the wall beside my bed. Peering over to my husband, I let out a small, indignant giggle. He is sleeping through this racket.

"When you asked me, I was so caught off-guard by it that I chose to lie to you. I mean, sis was in there with us." I swallowed. It was like choking down glass.

The longer we spoke, the more detail I could see of my father's face. His sad expression made me squint and turn away to fight back another wave of emotion. I felt the spirit cup my chin and turn my gaze back to him.

"I only wanted the truth out." The outline of his body softens, becoming more human and less like something from a horror film.

My mouth must have been agape. My teeth clatter as my jaw snaps shut.

"I had been talking to your grandmother. I'm afraid that your sister and mother overheard the conversation. They may have already known."

Anger flares within me. Out of respect, I breathe deep and pull that feeling back into control. Then I speak to make my point. "I wasn't ready."

"I see that now. Good intentions can still lead to mistakes. Even from the afterlife." He pauses in a way that begins to make me feel uncomfortable. "We all still love you, son. Your sisters and your mother should be proof enough of that."

I nod in agreement. "I have been lucky. I still hear of atrocities committed against people like me."

"It's getting better. It will take a while."

Again, I concur with his sentiment. An awful thought scrunches my face. It must have been a comical change. Laughter rumbles at the sudden switch of expression.

"Am I dead?"

He grasps me. The touch is both chilling and warm.

"Not yet. I'm not here to collect you."

I exhale, the breath cloudy from the visitor. Relief washes over me.

"I should go." Turning his eyes to mine, the moonlight flashes over his spectacles. My father reached for my cheek, wiping away the last of my tears, as he had when I was a boy when I skinned my knee.

"I'm so proud of you, son." He smirks; that touch of ornery in his smile that I was always far too familiar with. "And cut down on the sweets."

I match my expression to his. Genetics gave us that much in common. "Says the guy who sneaked jelly donuts."

"Look where it got me. I love you. Live your life knowing that."

I watch as he evaporates into the night, his touch on my face lingering. I bring my hand up to meet the spot, to hold that feeling there for as long as I can, to savor his final words.

As the cold visitor left, I sat on the edge of the bed, contemplating the night. Another hand caresses my back, causing me to emit a surprised yelp. I realize that it's my husband, turning over and looking at me with groggy eyes.

"Who were you talking to?"

"A visitor. It's nothing." I lower myself down to the bed, shake the sheets back over me, and kiss his hand. I know that tomorrow will bring a longer conversation.

Tonight, I drift back to sleep, worn through emotions. I rest, knowing that I am surrounded by love. Most importantly, I slumber, knowing that my regrets are forgiven and unfounded.

ACKNOWLEDGEMENTS

Despite how terrifying the journey may be for a writer to go from a spark of a concept to a finished product, it is a journey never taken alone. There are many people I'd like to thank for making the book you hold in your hand possible.

Foremost, I wish to thank my critique group for their unending support. Anika Hickman, Amanda Worthington, Christienne Gillispie, Brianna Privet, and Bridgette Henry all deserve my gratitude for their suggestions and improvements. Even though he isn't in the group, I'd also like to add J. Rocky Colavito to this list, since I assailed him on numerous occasions with these tales in exchange for his thoughts.

I want to thank Ruth Anna Evans for the wonderful cover she put together. It looks amazing!

Next, I want to give a shout out to my beta team, Dion Smith, Hope Amos, and Mark Runte. As with the above mentioned, this wouldn't have been possible without your valuable input. Thank you all so much.

And finally, I want to thank my husband, Brian, my family, friends, coworkers, the horror community in general, and of course, my dear readers, for being so supportive of my career.

Yes, I know I should be making money at it to truly call it a "career," but let's not peel the curtain back too far. I'm having fun. I hope my readers are as well.

<u>**Find other stories by Dan B. Fierce:**</u>

"Warning Shot," "Mistaken," and "Revenge"
The 2020 Indie Authors' Short Story Anthology, edited and curated by Mustang Patty (Heathory Press)

"Abandoned Bikes"
Clues and Culprits: An Anthology By the Indie Author's Group, edited and curated by Mustang Patty (Heathory Press)

"El Cangrejo"
HorrorScope, Vol. 1, edited by H. Everend (January Ember Press)

"Take Me to Church"
We're Here: An Anthology of LGBTQ+ Horror, edited by James G. Carlson (Gloom House Publishing)

"Hobo Nickel"
Cursed Items Anthology, edited and curated by Alisha McAdoo (Aye Alba Anthologies)

"The Void Screams Back"
Crazy from the Heat, edited and curated by Christopher Pelton (Psychotoxin Press)

"Roadkill King," by Dan B. Fierce (Fierce Imagination)

"Jamie Dice"
Winding Paths, Edited by Frances Pai Ippolito and Ken Hueler

"The Fledgling"
That Old House – The Bathroom Part Two, edited by Voices from the Mausoleum

"Accessorize"
Spectral Spectrum, Wicked House Press

ABOUT THE AUTHOR

Dan B. Fierce lives in his hometown of Kansas City, Missouri, with his husband of twenty-plus years and his family. He loves horror, comedy, and many things in between.

He has contributed short stories to many anthologies, all of which can be found on Amazon, Godless, and other digital or physical means.

This is his second solo publication.